EPIPHANY

STANLEY SYKES

The Reading Glass Books
1-888-420-3050
www.readingglassbooks.com
fulfillment@readingglassbooks.com

Contents

The Never-Ending War

Since the day of my birth, all I've known is war and survival. In my world, nothing else exists. Our pleasures are short-lived, and each day is spent finding new hiding places from our enemies. They are relentless—always developing new weapons to kill us. Our war has gone on for so long that no one can remember when it began.

It is said that we have always outnumbered them. When they discovered we could not be wiped out by brute force, they started making their weapons of war. Throughout our history, we have been persecuted. Why? Because we have no loftier goals than to eat, find shelter, and procreate. Are these not our inalienable rights? No one knows for sure.

For centuries, our only victory has been that we outnumber them. Our numbers are infinite. Kill us by the thousands and a thousand more will take their place. Our biological makeup is such that we become immune to their weapons after several exposures. So we lose countless tribesmen, women, and children each day. By the end of each life cycle, we are one billion strong again. So they try out new weapons, and we hide and survive, scrounging what scraps of food they leave behind and seeking shelter from harm.

So it has been for centuries before my time, and so it will be for centuries after, or so we thought.

They know we avoid light as much as possible, so they leave traps for us in the night. Most of these we just avoid, but some still attract us due to our hunger. That is how my parents died.

***

It was late one night, and they picked up the scent of food. I was half awake when I felt our link expand. I knew they had left our hiding place. I was drifting back to sleep when I heard their screams in my mind. As the rest of our tribe awoke, I raced to where my parents' screams had originated. It was too late for them.

They were caught in one of our enemies' housing simulations. It looked like one of their housing complexes except that it was on our scale. On the outside, it looked normal, but once inside, you were caught on a sticky, sweet-smelling substance that covered the floor. You didn't die right away. Depending on how you were stuck, you either starved to death or suffocated. The more you struggled, the more you became covered in the glue-like substance.

For those who were caught like that, there was no hope. They could not even be integrated back into the tribe by allowing it to be replenished on their remains. I learned a hard lesson that day.

We learned to avoid such traps, so the gassings began. After wiping out one or two generations, they became aware that we were adapting. Our numbers began to swell again. We became arrogant and stopped hiding from the light. We began to think that given enough time, we could literally overrun them. We became so relaxed that we didn't maintain our tribal links.

We thought we would go on forever. Until yesterday. Until the sky exploded with a blinding white light. I awoke this morning, alone. The air was hot, and I was burned.

As I got myself together, I realized that the link was severed. Dazed, I looked around to see burned and charred bodies everywhere. The enemy had finally triumphed. They were all dead. Billions of bodies carpeted the land. How? What had they done? I had no answers. All I knew was that I was utterly alone. Wait! There was a faint nudge of awareness. Someone somewhere had also survived. I must find them, no matter where I must go. The enemies thought they had finally won, wiped out all the—what did they call us?—roaches.

Once I rest, find food, and heal, I will find the other survivors.

We will begin anew. The war is not yet over.

The Elevator

My name is Richard Pierce. I used to work for a state mental facility. Now I reside in one. No one believes me. They can't explain the strange things that happened, so I was their scapegoat. I write this down in the hope that someone will read this and see the truth.

***

It started about six months ago. I was working as a therapy aide at Cypress Psychiatric Center. There were tales about ghosts and such throughout the hospital. After being there for four years, I chalked it up to gossip and something to throw a scare into newbies. Then something happened.

It was wintertime, and we were getting snow off and on. The facility had large grounds. It was made up of three large buildings, the administration building and two buildings to house the patients. Building A was where they housed the short-term patients—those who can make the transition to a group home or family or who can function on their own with meds and therapy. Building B was for the long-term patients—the ones who are unstable or unable to function normally in society. It was Saturday, and I was working overtime. I was escorting a patient from building A to building B.

The client was telling me that he just couldn't cope with outside life anymore. Then we heard someone screaming. I looked across the grass and saw a female staff member running from building B, screaming and crying. As she got closer, I recognized Ms. Brown. She'd been there for about a year. I grabbed her and asked her to calm down and tell me what happened. She kept saying "Oh my god, his head" over and over. I thought it would be best if I took her and Mr. Johnson back to building A. As we walked back, she finally calmed down enough to tell me what happened.

She and a coworker, a Mr. Long, got on the elevator on the eighteenth floor to come downstairs on their break. When the car reached the thirteenth floor, it suddenly stopped. "The door opened," she said, "but no one got on." After a few minutes, the door remained open. That was when Mr. Long decided to take a look, thinking someone was playing games. No sooner had he poked his head out to see what was going on when the door slammed shut. She said that the force was so great that it shook the entire elevator and took his head completely off. In a state of shock, she watched his body collapse to the floor, spurting blood from his headless neck. The door opened and closed quickly, and then the elevator brought them down to the first floor. When the door opened, she ran screaming from the elevator past whoever was in the lobby.

After we entered the lobby of building A, I called security. I told her to tell the officers what she had told me. I also asked her to look after Mr. Johnson while I went back to building B.

As I entered the lobby, I could see Mr. Long's body lying on the floor. It was covered by a bloody sheet. Not far from him, I could see the inside of the elevator, the walls and floor covered with blood. Bloody footprints ran from the elevator to the front door. I stopped to talk to the security officer standing by the body. She told me that two of her coworkers had gone upstairs to retrieve Mr. Long's head. I chatted with her for a few minutes, then I took my leave. I headed back to building A. As I walked back, I thought to myself, *A freak accident, nothing more.* But as these thoughts ran through my mind, the hairs on the back of my neck stood up. Little did I know, this was just the beginning.

For the next few days, Mr. Long's death was the talk of the hospital. The elevator was shut down and inspected numerous times. They could find nothing wrong mechanically. After a week or so, it was back to business. The elevator was running again, and no one seemed apprehensive about using it. There were whispers about spirits and such from patients and old-time staffers. But for the most part, people accepted the idea that it was a freak accident. That was until two days after the funeral.

There were twenty floors in building B, with four wards on each floor. They were designated ward 5A, 5B, etc., on up to the eighteenth floor. Floors 19 and 20 were supplies and storage, respectively.

Two days after Mr. Long's funeral, a group of patients were being escorted to the treatment mall. The treatment mall was located in building A, on the second and third floors. Two TAs and eight patients got on the elevator. One of the TAs stated later that as soon as the doors closed, the elevator literally dropped toward the main floor. From what I was told, it hit the main floor with such force that it shattered most of the windows. When the doors opened, one TA fell out, landing flat on his back, hitting his head. He suffered a concussion. Three of the patients broke an arm or a leg. The other TA and the rest of the patients were huddled in a corner, in shock. EMS was called, and all parties were rushed to the hospital.

For two weeks, the elevator was out of use, as repairmen inspected it from top to bottom. I talked to some of the staff who managed to speak to the repairmen. They said the repairmen were stumped as to the cause of the incident. They couldn't find anything wrong with the elevator. That's when the whispers about the spirits of dead patients began again. The old stories about clients who died and strange happenings resurfaced.

For a month or so after it was deemed operational, clients refused to ride in the elevator. The staff member who suffered the concussion was out on compensation. The staff member who went into shock quit a week after the incident. Things seemed to return back to normal. Then, it happened.

I had just returned from pass. As I signed in, I was told I had to float to ward 13A in building B. I was apprehensive, but I couldn't refuse without a legitimate reason. So I went to my ward first and changed into my sweats and lab coat. I then proceeded to my assignment. As I walked to building B, I had my pocket flashlight on, looking out for skunks that roamed the grounds at night. Once I was in the lobby, I remembered how empty and spooky this building felt. At night, it always felt eerie there, as if you were cut off from the rest of the world. After pushing those thoughts from my mind, I took a deep breath and got on the elevator. I took out my keys, inserted the 141 key into the control panel, and pushed 13. I silently prayed that nothing odd would happen. Nothing did. I stepped off the elevator and let out a sigh of relief.

When I opened the door to ward 13A, the odor hit me in the face—a smell of urine, feces, vomit, and body odor all mixed together. Most wards had an atmosphere all their own, some worse than others. I locked the door and walked down the hall to the nursing station. Upon entering, I recognized the other staff members: Mr. Rodriguez, whom I trained with, and Ms. Brown. She was the staff member who witnessed the first incident. The nurse, Ms. Trang, was making out the assignment sheet. We all exchanged greetings, and I sat down. All the regular staff, including the nurse, had been calling in for the past month or so. Even though all the strange occurrences had happened in the daytime, no one wanted to work in this building at night.

Nurse Trang, like most of the nurses in the hospital, knew that I didn't sleep. So she gave me the four to seven rounds. She said there were no observations, so it should be a quiet night. After everyone looked at the assignment sheet, I informed the nurse that I wanted to go downstairs to get something from the vending machines. She said "All right," and I left the ward. I was lost in thought, and my heart leaped into my throat when the elevator stopped with a jolt between the sixth and fifth floors. My mind started racing, then it started up again. After I got my snacks, I had second thoughts about riding back upstairs. All of a sudden, the lights went out in the lobby. I managed to keep my wits about me and took out my flashlight. I waited to see if the emergency lights would come on. Two minutes later, the lights came back on. I decided it would be best if I got back upstairs as quick as possible. I said a silent prayer and got back on the elevator. When I got off on the thirteenth floor, I thanked God nothing had happened.

This time, when I opened the ward door, a different odor hit me. The coppery smell of blood permeated the air. I quickly locked the door as I noticed all the lights were out. I took out my flashlight and proceeded down the hall slowly, listening for the slightest sound. I wondered where my coworkers were, so I checked the nursing station first. The emergency lights made the place look surreal. Both doors were locked, and the staff was nowhere to be seen. I opened the door to the treatment room, and that thick coppery smell almost made me gag. Ms. Trang was the first one I saw as I shone my flashlight directly into the room.

There she was, pinned against the wall next to the eye chart. She looked like a butterfly in a collection, except she was three feet off the floor. Syringes pierced her flesh and bone, holding her up. Her head was on backward. Whatever food I had left inside me from lunch came up as I turned to the sink opposite the door. I started to rinse my mouth when I noticed something out of the corner of my eye. Sitting up in the corner was the body of Ms. Brown. Her head had been squeezed as if it were a melon. Both her eyes were dangling from their sockets, and her tongue had been torn out. It was lying in her lap.

I slowly scanned the room, looking for whoever might have done this, but I saw no one. I wondered where Rodriguez was. I tried using the payphone, but it didn't work. We weren't allowed to bring our cell phones on the wards.

The realization hit me that I had to check the patients. Part of me just wanted to walk off the ward and go for help, but I couldn't. If some of the patients had done this, then I had to ensure the safety of the others. I headed back toward the front door to start checking the dorms. Halfway down the hall, I was stopped in my tracks by a scream that sent chills down my spine. It sounded as if it came from the dayroom.

As I walked back, it was followed by another scream and another. I quickened my pace, and it suddenly got quiet. When I reached the dayroom, I noticed the door was locked. Since there were no lights on in there, I shone my flashlight through the window. What I saw would give me nightmares for the rest of my life.

Whatever had done this, it wasn't the patients. The patients were in the dayroom, all of them all over the dayroom. There were body parts everywhere. I tried to open the door to see if anyone was still alive, but it wouldn't budge. I trained my flashlight down to the floor in front of the door and saw why.

Mr. Rodriguez's body, along with several others', was blocking the door. I needed two things then, something to break the window with and a weapon. I went back into the treatment room and removed the blade on the old paper cutter. Then I went into the nursing station and took the fire extinguisher from its hooks on the wall. I went back to the dayroom.

It took several swings, but I managed to break one of the wired glass panes out. After removing the jagged edges of glass that remained, I climbed into the dayroom. The stench was unbearable; blood, feces, urine, internal organs, and body parts littered the floor. Some of the clients were flung against the windows, busted open, or smashed. One female client was spread-eagled on the floor, an old- fashioned blood pressure gauge protruding from her vagina. I was going to be sick again, but I held it down.

In the corner near the female bathroom, I saw what had done this. It looked like the embers of a dying fire. The only thing was that these embers or glowing sparks weren't burning. What they were doing was ripping through and ripping apart a patient. As if sensing my presence, they started coming toward me. Backing away, I kept swinging the blade in front of me. Seeing that it did no good, I dropped it and leaped through the dayroom window. Once I hit the floor, I ran, pulling out my keys as I headed for the door. The door now opened; I just closed it behind me, not bothering to lock it. I ran for the elevator. After I got on, I must have passed out. That is how security and the police found me about half an hour later. They said I was covered in blood and was babbling about some strange lights. I awoke in the hospital, strapped to a bed. The following day, the police came to arrest me. They said all thirty-three clients were dead, along with two staff members and the nurse.

The next few weeks were a blur, as I went back and forth from the hospital to court. The newspapers said I was the worst mass murderer the city had ever seen. They said I had snapped a case of occupational burnout. They showed gruesome pictures taken at the scene. As evidence, they had the blade with my fingerprints on it, as well as bloodstains.

***

So that's my story. They can't explain the incidents that led up to that night or why no one heard any screams or cries for help as the victims were being hacked to death.

Here I am, in a hospital for the criminally insane, where I will probably spend the rest of my life, unless somebody believes me.

The End?

Reflections

Prologue

Little Zack was just like any normal eight-year-old. He loved watching cartoons, playing video games, getting dirty, and eating junk food. He liked school and had several friends, whom he enjoyed playing with.

His favorite pastime though was playing grown-up in the mirror. Alone in his room, he would stare into his dresser mirror and dictate orders to his reflection. He liked the feeling of being in charge. Tonight was no different.

He stood on his chair in front of his dresser and barked orders at his reflection.

To his surprise, his reflection crossed its arms and said no! Before Zack could utter a scream, two strong little arms reached through the mirror and . . .

Reflections

It's Sunday, May 2, and I should be at home asleep. My name is Steve Taylor. I'm considered the black sheep of my family. I've been arrested and had dealings with militant groups, and I've dabbled here and there in the occult.

You can imagine my surprise when I received a phone call at one in the morning. It was my brother-in-law. He said my nephew Zack was missing and that I should come right away. I asked to speak with my sister, Ann. He said the doctor had given her a sedative.

I said "All right" and hung up the phone.

The drive to Pennsylvania was eight hours, so I packed a few things and headed out. Before leaving the city though, I stopped at an ATM and withdrew some cash to tide me over. That was three hours ago.

During the drive, I had time to ponder the situation. I haven't seen Zack in over a year. It's his father's doing, no doubt. I never liked Robert and didn't hesitate in letting it be known.

My sister once told me that if I couldn't be civil to him, I shouldn't come around.

Zack, on the other hand, was a lot like me. He wanted to know why—why people treated one another so poorly, why God let terrible things happen, and why we were here.

Robert concluded that I was a bad influence on his son. My sister tried to stay neutral for the most part. She didn't approve of my lifestyle, but she knew that I was a survivor. She didn't mind my imparting that to her son.

The question that kept popping up in my mind was, Why me? What did they need me there for? I guess I'd just have to wait and find out.

Four and a half hours later, I pulled up to the house. I parked behind a police car. A cop approached me as I was getting out of my car and asked who I was. I told him who I was and showed him my ID. I asked him what the story was. He said that I should talk to the detectives inside. As I started up the steps, with the cop in tow, the front door opened. Robert came out and thanked me for getting there so soon.

After going inside, we all took seats in the living room. Robert offered me something to drink, and I told him, "Coffee, black with sugar." I had a feeling it was going to be a long day. As Robert went into the kitchen to make my coffee, the detectives turned their attention to me.

One of the detectives, a well-built large man in his late thirties, stood up and introduced himself. "My name is Detective Jay Reynolds, and my partner is Detective Smith."

I introduced myself and asked what they would like to know.

Detective Reynolds asked me when was the last time I saw Zack. I told him a little over a year ago. He asked if Zack had written to me or called, and I said "Not lately." I explained that I had been out of the country for the past six months on business and just returned two weeks ago. While this discourse was going on, I observed his partner taking notes.

Robert came back in at this time and sat a tray down on the coffee table. He took the cup of coffee off the tray and handed it to me. The fact that he did so amused me.

My sister thought that my main reason for disliking Robert was that he was white. In actuality, I disliked him because he was a snobbish, pompous ass, one of those people born into money, who thought the world revolved around them. I was able to put my prejudices aside because my sister loved him.

Now back to the matter at hand.

Detective Reynolds asked for my current address in case they had more questions for me. I told him what he wanted to know and turned to Robert. I politely asked him what the hell had happened to Zack. After giving me a look of indignation, he filled in the blanks.

***

Thursday after dinner, about 8:00 p.m., Zack began his usual routine for a school night. He went upstairs to brush his teeth and changed into his pajamas. Then he'd spend about ten or fifteen minutes talking to himself in his mirror. He didn't know I knew this. I caught him one night, just as I was about to come and tuck him in. Anyway, I figured I'd check the bathroom first. The door was closed, so I knocked. No answer. I opened the door and went in. On the sink lay his toothbrush, toothpaste, and washcloth, but no Zack. Feeling a sense of dread, I rushed to his bedroom. The door was open, the light was on, but no Zack. I called down to my wife and asked if Zack was with her. She said no as she hurried upstairs, asking what was wrong.

I told her he was missing. She ran into his room, calling his name. When after threats of punishment no Zack came out, she ran into our bedroom and called the police.

We were instructed not to touch anything and wait for the detectives to arrive. Then, I called EMS after she went into hysterics. After they gave her a sedative to calm her down, I called you.

***

As the detectives were preparing to leave, I told Robert I wanted to have a look at Zack's room and the bathroom. He said, "What the hell for?"

This caught the detectives' attention, and they turned back to approach us. When they asked if everything was all right, Robert had sense enough to reply yes. He was just upset over today's events, he said. After explaining to Robert the procedure for a possible kidnapping, they left.

After I told Robert why I wanted to examine the bathroom, I went out to my car. I opened the trunk and took out a small duffle bag. I went back into the house.

Robert asked what was inside the bag. I told him they were tools to help me find out if something out of the norm had occurred. I left the bathroom and went into Zack's room. It took me about fifteen minutes to confirm what I had suspected since Robert told us what happened. A door had been opened into our world, and my nephew was taken through it.

The Observer

It was a quiet afternoon in Bryant Park. Like most Saturdays, the park was filled with tourists and their children, trying to escape the July heat and relax. Single women were sitting and reading or talking on their cell phones. Couples were pushing strollers while leisurely walking by.

I was sitting and listening to my CD player when the incident began. It started as a rumbling underneath the pavement, barely noticeable since the subway was at the corner of the park.

It was about a quarter after four when the vibrations began to grow stronger. The walkways in the park consisted of large and small rectangular and square concrete slabs. As the vibrations grew stronger, the slabs began to shift. Chairs started falling over, and people began to panic. Mothers ran to snatch their kids off the carousel as it too began to tilt from side to side.

This lasted about fifteen minutes, and then it abruptly stopped. No more rumblings, no more vibrations. In that moment, it was as if a vacuum had sucked up all the air out of the park. No one uttered a sound; people just stared at one another in disbelief.

Then, without warning, the horror began. "Things" started bursting through the concrete and pulling people into the ground. At first, all you could hear was the tearing of earth and the shattering of concrete as two, three, and a dozen broke through. Then the screams drowned out everything else. Four of the things grabbed the carousel from different sides and pulled it into the ground. Luckily, there were no children on it.

No other inanimate object was touched, except for the chairs and tables that were knocked over as the things broke free.

Less than a dozen people made it out of the park alive. I was one of the last people questioned by the police. They arrived about five minutes after the strange occurrence stopped, along with EMS.

All the survivors were treated for shock. A few were so traumatized they had to be hospitalized.

***

It is now a week later. The park has been blocked off and quarantined. Mine was the only lucid account of what transpired. Being a writer, I am always noticing details.

Although our stories mirrored one another, only I was able to describe what those things looked like. The authorities dismissed that part of my story as the ramblings of someone suffering from post-traumatic stress. But I will never forget what I observed that day.

The things that burst forth from the earth that day were as wide as the trees themselves. They resembled roots, except they were of a greenish-gray hue and covered in yellowish slime. The strangest thing of all though was what appeared to be little mouths down the center of the things. The edges of the things were covered with barbs about an inch wide and two inches long. They resembled some kind of grotesque tentacles.

It is only now, a week later, that I begin to make some sense of the occurrence. We have all heard, in fairy tales and fantasies, of earth spirits, guardians of the forests and trees.

What if what I saw were indeed the arms of some hellish creature down in the bowels of the earth? What if nature is fighting back against the atrocities done to her? What if I am not mad, as the authorities suggest, and this is just the beginning?

A Day in the Life of a Sociopath

My name is Robert. It's eight o'clock at night, and my day is about to begin. I work at night, so my day begins at 11:00 p.m. The end is near. Soon, the facade will be gone, and the dark one will emerge again. So I must write down my thoughts and feelings for posterity,

for soon I will no longer care.

For years, I have played the role, blended in like a chameleon. No one suspects, and no one sees that change is about to occur. I work in a hospital, with others like myself. The clients don't know how much we have in common. My normality is almost perfect. Almost, because every now and then, the lights go out in my eyes and the dark one tries to emerge. But I have become very skilled at keeping him in check. My coworkers sense a difference in me, but we all have our little quirks.

Even the woman I loved didn't suspect the truth. She's gone now, taken away by an uncaring fool. She died recently, and my humanity went with her.

So with my last bit of sanity, I try to let the world at large know what it's in for.

As I ride the train to work, I observe the people around me. I look at the couples who seem so happy together, and I feel a longing in my heart for my love.

And I remember watching her go through the years of pain and suffering, mostly from her peers. She never knew that I absorbed it all, felt all the hurt, and cried inside as she died inside.

Soon the pain will be replaced by a blackness that knows no remorse, that is unforgiving.

I observe three teenagers getting on the train, males sporting their gang colors. I think to myself, *How easy it would be to erase them from the face of the earth.* They think in terms of guns and box cutters when it comes to hurting someone. If only they knew the exquisite pleasure of puncturing a main artery and watching your adversary bleed to death or breaking twenty or thirty of their bones and watching as they wished they were dead. Soon they will all know that they cannot escape, for it begins tonight.

The ride to work is uneventful, as always. Tonight would have been my night off, but my plan called for me to be there. A week ago, I had arranged a work adjustment with someone so I could work tonight. My prey, as it were, will be on her ward tonight, and so will I. As I sign in, I observe that no one notices me, which is very favorable. I go up to my own ward first to get something from my locker. I take out the syringe filled with Haldol and place it in a small plastic bag. This and a few other items I place in my refreshment bag, along with my coffee cup, sugar, etc. Then I head downstairs to my assigned ward for the night.

After I enter the ward, I check to see who the nurse is for the night. Although their habits seldom vary, I leave nothing to chance. Upon entering the nursing station, I give the expected greeting and find myself a seat. There is some light conversation, and I give an occasional nod or a yes here and there. Most of the talk is between Ms. N. and Ms. C. The other staff member, Mr. R., is down the hall, sitting with an arm's length observation.

I can't help but marvel at how easy it is to blend in and hardly be noticed at the same time. As the conversation drags on, I check out the assignment sheet. As I knew I would be, I am assigned to do the laundry. I have the last two hours with the one to one, and my lunch break is at two thirty. Be still, my heart. Everything is falling into place nicely.

I get up and excuse myself. I head for the linen room to get the stretcher ready for the laundry. As I'm walking down the hall back to the nursing station, I hear Ms. N. tell her partner that she doesn't trust me. I stop and listen, making a mental note to staple her lips together, *later*.

Ms. C. comments that she doesn't have a problem with me. Ms. N. states that she is afraid to be alone with me. Neither of them realizes that I'm standing right by the door, listening to every word. I clear my throat and startle both of them, especially Ms. N. The little pleasures are sometimes the best.

It's now a little after one, and I tell them I'm going downstairs to the vending machines. I ask if anyone wants anything, and they both say no (no doubt glad to get rid of me for a while). On the way downstairs, I think about my love and how much I miss her and how she'll have plenty of company, real soon! I take my time so as not to deviate from my normal routine.

As I come back on the ward, I check my watch. I see it's almost one thirty, time to put my plan into action. Ms. C. has retired to the dayroom to watch the tape I so generously provided. Ms. N. is still in the nursing station, reading a magazine.

As I enter, I ask Ms. N. where I can go to smoke a cigarette without having to go back downstairs. Since I know she smokes, what better way to bait my trap. She reluctantly agrees to show me since she wants to smoke too. I tell her I'll let Ms. C. know, and I'll meet her at the door.

I inform Ms. C. that I'm going to smoke and that I'll be back shortly. I stop back in the nursing station to get some things from my bag and lock the door. The smoking room is situated at the other end of the hall, between two other wards.

As we walk down the hall, she tells me that she's sorry about the passing of my lady friend.

I smile and say thank you. All the while, I know that she couldn't care less. A smile is a wonderful thing. It can express joy, love, and happiness, or it can hide pain, loneliness, or the blackest of souls. I learned this from my love.

Once we are in the smoking room, she asks me for a light. I reach into my pocket for what she thinks is my lighter and pull out the syringe. As her eyes fly open in astonishment, I plunge the needle into her jugular vein. In one swift movement, I cover her mouth with one hand and push down the plunger of the syringe with the other. The drug will take about three minutes to incapacitate her. I know, because I field-tested it a week ago.

Once she's knocked out, I remove my hand from her mouth and gently place her in a chair. Then I reach into my lab coat pocket and pull out the half pint of vodka I purchased for this occasion. I open the bottle and go to the window, where I pour out about one-quarter of the bottle. I go back to her and tilt her head back so I can pour some of the alcohol into her mouth. I make sure not to pour it too fast or pour too much so that she'll involuntarily swallow it. I place the bottle in her lap and leave.

I go back to the ward and get the stretcher for the laundry. I check my watch and see that fifteen minutes have passed since I went to smoke.

Right on time, I go to the dayroom and tell Ms. C. that I'm going to do the laundry. She nods okay and turns her attention back to the television. I roll the stretcher out into the hall and lock the ward door.

I head down the hall to the smoking room. I open the door, roll the stretcher inside, and lock the door. I lift up the sheet. I drape it over on one side and deposit Ms. N.'s body on the shelf underneath. I let the sheet back down and open the door. Now comes the hard part. As I roll the stretcher into the elevator, I check my watch. It is now two o'clock in the morning. By the time I get to the other building, it will be almost two fifteen. After I get off the elevator, I check the halls to make sure they are empty. I head for the corridor that leads to the other building. I stop when I reach it and check the halls again.

Satisfied that no one is around, I continue down the hall. I slow my pace as I get near the nursing office. The weight of the laundry and my passenger keeps the stretcher from making any unnecessary noise. Once past the doorway, I pick up my pace.

When I reach the end of the corridor, I make a right then head down another hallway toward the other building and the elevators. Since no patients are being housed on this side for the time being, it's smooth sailing from here on. I get on the elevator and pull out my keys. I insert my 141 key into the control panel and push 13. I check the time and see that it's two sixteen.

As I roll the stretcher off the elevator, I see that the long table is still where I left it last week. I lift up one side of the sheet and see that my passenger is still out. I bend down and gently lift her up and place her on the table. I feel underneath the table to make sure the restraints are still in place. I then strip off all her clothes. First, I restrain her hands and neck, then her feet. I take out my bag of tools from under the stretcher and place it on the table. I pull off the latex gloves and drop them into my bag.

I get back on the elevator with the stretcher. I check my watch again and see that it's two thirty. After I exit the elevator on the first floor, I stop and get a soda from the machine. Insurance, just in case someone should see me in the hall on my way to the other building. I carefully make my way back to the other building without incident. I take the elevator to my floor and head for the laundry room.

Once inside, I place the clothes in the machines and start them up. I take the stretcher and head back to the ward. I place the stretcher back in the linen room. I then go to the dayroom and tell Ms. C. that I'm going on my lunch break now.

Ms. C. asks me about Ms. N., and I tell her, "I think she's in the bathroom." I tell her that I'm going out with someone and ask if she wants anything. She says no, so I go and get my jacket and leave. I check my watch and see that it's two fifty-five. That gives me about an hour to take care of my business.

I go downstairs and head back to the other building. On the elevator ride up, I think about how Ms. N. had put my love's life in danger and threatened me. *Stupid bitch!* After I exit the elevator, I turn it off just to be on the safe side. I walk over to the table and pick up another pair of gloves. I put them on and check on my victim.

I open her eyes and see that the drug is starting to wear off. Since I can't afford to wait, I reach into my bag and pull out the small vial of ammonia that I hooked up for this occasion.

Before I wake her, I pull out the duct tape in the bag and tape her mouth. Now, no one can hear her screams. I uncap the vial, lift her head, and place it under her nose. A few good whiffs and her eyes pop open. She looks around and tries to focus. Then she looks up at me, and you can see the terror in her eyes. I tell her not to worry. "You're not going to die right away. Your punishment is to suffer first. I'm going to make you wish I had killed you. No one knows where you are, and by the time they find you, I'll be gone. Did you know that for most of my adolescent years and adult life, I had recurring dreams about being stabbed or sliced up? Groups of people with knives or razors would attack me. Do you know how I overcame that fear? I learned to use sharp objects—knives, razors, nails, ice picks, pins, etc.—as if I were a surgeon. And you will have the pleasure of

witnessing my skill firsthand."

That said, I reach into my bag and pull out four vials of Chinese liniment for toughening the skin.

"This may sting," I say as I put on two more pairs of examination gloves. "It will make the process go faster," I explain as I rub her down from head to toe. "In case you're wondering what I'm going to do, it's simple. I'm going to skin you alive." I pull off the gloves and replace them with three fresh pairs. Then I go to work.

The hardest part is flipping her over, with all the blood making her hard to grip. Forty-five minutes later, it is done. I have to revive her about five times throughout the ordeal. Now I am ready to add the finishing touch. Reaching once more into my bag, I pull out two fifteen-ounce spray bottles. They are filled with saltwater, lemon juice, and honey mixture.

"Too bad I can't let you scream out loud," I say. "It would have been a heartwarming sound. Before I go, I'll grant you one wish. I know your body is burning, being raw. So I'll spray you down with this water to relieve some of your pain." I start from her feet and work my way up. You can tell by the way her body trembles, as she pulls against the restraints, that it is having the desired effect.

I think her eyes are going to pop out when I reach her vagina and then her breasts. Now that would have been exquisite. I begin packing up my tools then. After making sure I leave nothing behind, I take a few moments to examine my handiwork.

The hardest part had been her head, which I mercifully did while she was unconscious. I had to cut her ears off in order to peel her scalp down and back. The eyelids presented a minor problem, so I did them first. To make sure she wouldn't mess me up by squirming around or refusing to close her eyes, I pinned her eyelids in place with four pushpins I took from my lab coat pocket. Then I made an incision from one corner of the eyelid to the other. I gently lifted up the skin (the first layer) and pulled it off. Just before it was almost off, I paused to see the fear in her pleading eyes. Then I yanked it off, feeling much pleasure as her body squirmed and shook. I wanted her to suffer!

But enough reminiscing. It is time to go. I turn to her and say, "Like Jerry Springer, I leave you with this parting thought. You're not dead yet, and even when the bugs and rodents finish your torture, you'll live, maybe. Unless your heart just can't take any more and gives up. In any case, you reap what you sow. I know you're thinking so will I, but guess what, it doesn't matter, because I'm dead already. By the time they find you, you'll either be dead or insane. A win-win situation for me. Not to worry though. Before I'm done, you'll have plenty of company."

With that, I pick up my bag of tools and take the elevator downstairs. I stop the elevator on the tenth floor and remove my bloody clothes. After changing into the clothes I left there a week ago, I place them in a plastic bag.

I then put that in a laundry bag. I stop in the lobby of the main building and call up to the ward. After about six rings or so, Ms. C. picks up the phone. I tell her it's me and that I'll be back on the ward after I check on the clothes. I ask her if she found Ms. N., and she says no. I say "That figures" and hung up the phone. Ten minutes later, I'm back on the ward. It is now four thirty. I wait until five o clock, then I get up and go see the nurse.

I explain to her that Ms. N. is not on the ward and that she's been gone a long time. She goes into the dayroom to ask Ms. C. if she knows where she went. She comes out of the dayroom with the nurse and states that I was the last one who saw her.

I say, "Given our history, do you really think I know where she went?"

Ms. C. whispers to the nurse for about three minutes, and the nurse says, "Oh!" The nurse says that if she's not back on the ward by six o'clock, she'll inform the administrator downstairs. I state that if she were me, she'd be on the phone already. Before she could respond, I say, "I'm going to check on the laundry."

At six, the nurse makes the call downstairs. At six fifteen, the nurse administrator comes up on the ward. He questions Ms. C. and me, then he confers with the nurse. As he and the nurse start walking down the hall toward the door, I exclaim that she's probably drunk someplace. The NA stops in his tracks and calls me to him. He tells me that I am very unprofessional in making such a statement. He says that I should keep my opinions to myself. I say "Fine" and walk away. By seven forty-five, I'm on my way home. I am very pleased at a job well done. No more holding back, no more turning the other cheek. Finally, it has begun!

Shadow Master

My name is Anthony Afina. I'm a defense attorney. Most of my clients are of dubious nature—drug dealers, mafioso, you name it. I'm now on my way to see one such client.

I met him for the first time seven months ago at One Police Plaza. He made the news big-time. The newspapers called him Shadow Master. His real name is Charles Damon. The media called him the "demon killer," emphasis on demon. He was charged with the deaths of two hundred and fifty people. It wasn't the number of people as much as the gruesome ways they died and that he allegedly killed them all at the same time. Even in the year 2010, that seemed an impossible feat.

As I pulled up to the pier where the ferry was waiting, I couldn't help but wonder if he was the head of some insane cult. Maybe his followers killed all those people and somehow managed to leave without being seen. I would find out soon enough.

On the ferry ride to Randall's Island Max Security Prison, I went over my briefs and started writing down the important questions. At the dock on the island, a car was waiting for me on the other side of an electric fence. There were no guards here, just two security cameras over the locked doorway and a handprint box on either side of the door. I pressed my palm up against the handprint box and waited.

Ten seconds later, there was a clicking sound, and the door swung open. The driver of the car got out and stood on the passenger side. When I got to the car, he frisked me, and then he told me to place my briefcase on the roof of the car and to open it. He gestured for me to back away, all the while showing me the nine-millimeter holstered at his waist. He briefly but methodically searched the contents of the case then closed it and tossed it on the backseat. Then he gestured for me to get in.

The prison was built on the side of the island facing the water. It was circumvented by another electric fence. Between the pier and the prison, there were housing facilities and two other buildings. One housed the generators, which supplied the electricity. The other one was for equipment and supplies. After repeating the identification process, I was led into a security office where the chief of security waited.

"Good morning, Mr. Afina. My name is Captain Wills." He shook my outstretched hand and asked me to have a seat. "I understand you're here to see prisoner Damon."

I said yes and allowed him to continue.

"As you have been informed, he is in a special containment area built especially for him. Since you are his lawyer, I have been instructed to show you a video tape from the office building where the murders took place. I must warn you though. What you're about to see, no one outside of the chief of police, the DA, the warden, and myself has seen." He then picked up a remote control and turned the television on. He pushed the tape into the VCR, and it came on and started to play.

The room that came into view looked like a convention hall. It was full of chairs, tables, and people. From the angle being shown, the video camera was at the back of the room, by the entrance. At the front of the room was a podium, where someone was speaking. The people sitting at the tables looked like executives, men and women dressed in business suits, sipping coffee and chatting. Occasionally, you could see them applaud as the speakers finished and changed. There was no audio—thank God!—for this went on for about half an hour.

Suddenly, everyone's head turned toward the door. A man entered and walked down the middle aisle toward the podium. You couldn't see his face, but it was clear that he and the speaker knew each other. The look on the speaker's face was one of outrage. The man stopped about halfway down the aisle. By the gestures and the look on the speaker's face, you could tell that they exchanged words, angry words. The man turned then and spoke to the people sitting at the tables. As he turned, you could see that it was my client, Mr. Charles Damon. Suddenly, the looks on people's faces went from bewilderment to sheer terror. People started running for the door, as others were being torn apart, torn apart by what appeared to be shadows—shadows of wild animals, monsters, inhuman grotesque things, and things from nightmares. And in the midst of it all stood my client. When it was all over, no one remained alive, except Charles Damon. There was blood everywhere, body parts, half-eaten torsos, and headless, faceless, and limbless corpses. The shadow creatures disappeared, as if they never existed. Only my client was alive, standing there, surveying the carnage. That's how the police found him. The tape ended.

I turned to the trash can next to me and heaved up my lunch. Captain Wills waited until I got myself together before he spoke. "What do you make of that?" he asked.

I was speechless.

"I worked fifteen years as a city cop before I took this position," he said, "and I never saw anything like this."

A couple of hours after he was booked, the chief of police got a strange phone call. He said a man claiming to be a doctor called him, saying he had information concerning Mr. Damon. "He called me half an hour later and asked me to prepare a special cell. He wouldn't elaborate as to why, but he might be willing to talk to you." Captain Wills then gave me the chief's private number and said he was expecting my call. He stood up then, saying it was time to take me to my client. As we walked down the corridor toward the cellblock where my client was, I remembered the day I met him.

***

He had just been booked and given his one phone call. After he told me his name, I asked him how he got my number. He said it was given to him by a former client of mine, whom he did some work for. I agreed to talk to him, and I told him I'd be there in about an hour. One hour and fifteen minutes later, we were sitting across each other in an interrogation room at One Police Plaza. My first question

to him was the obvious one, "Did you kill those people?"

His answer wasn't really an answer. "Do you really think I could have killed all those people?" he asked? His answer was typical of the client I usually deal with, but something in the way he said it made my neck hairs stood up.

My next question was, "Why should I take your case?"

He said, "Because it will probably be the biggest case of your life." He was probably right, but I wouldn't let him know it. After that,

I asked the customary background questions: Where do you live? Where do you work? Do you have a criminal history? And so forth. After writing down all the information, I stood up and told him to call me in two days and I'd let him know my decision. As I shook his hand, I got that feeling again. Even though he looked normal enough, something wasn't quite right.

***

That was seven months ago. After seeing that video tape, I knew why the DA was going to recommend no bail at the hearing tomorrow. Captain Wills was explaining why this prison was unique. I knew the history for the most part, so I tuned him out.

In the year 2002, the whole penal system for New York State changed. The new mayor, ex-President Clifton, said that he would make New York crime-free. His first proposal was to do away with juvenile institutions. Any crime done by a juvenile that called for doing time would be carried out in a real jail. His second proposal was that any time an adult was sentenced to more than three years, it would be straight time with no parole.

Tired of all the street crimes and the negative publicity, the police were constantly getting the governor and the senate passed both proposals unanimously. Any juvenile sentenced to jail time was sent upstate to Green Haven, Comstock, Napanock, or Woodburn. If their crime was murder, they stayed upstate until they were twenty-one. Then they were sent to Randall's Island to finish out their sentence. Mayor Clifton said that he would build the safest maximum security prison in the country. He said he wanted criminals in New York to know that if they broke the law, the consequences would be dire.

By 2007, he had his escape-proof prison. The guards had less contact with the prisoners due to the handprint boxes. When in the mess hall or the yard, the prisoners were let in by a guard and let out by a guard. Of the seven cellblocks, only two were let out for meals or exercise at the same time. The mess hall was equipped with video cameras so that if any altercation jumped off, the room was immediately pumped full of mace. The yard was equipped with cameras also, and motion detectors hooked up to .45-caliber machine guns. If a prisoner got too close to the fence, he might not live to talk about it. With two security fences, guards housed between the two, it was the perfect jail. From an aerial view, the prison was wheel-like in shape, the hub being the main building where the receiving area, clinic, warden's office, security offices, and communications were; the spokes being the corridors leading to the cellblocks; and the security fences making up the rim.

When Captain Wills and I reached the end of the corridor, we stopped instead of going through the doors to cellblock 4. Off to the side was an elevator, which we got on. We got off on what should have been the roof. Captain Wills explained that in order to accommodate the police chief, as far as his request, they literally had to add another floor to the cellblock. "We nicknamed this the Penthouse," he said, "for if what we suspect about your client is true, he's only the first." It looked like a hospital ward.

About fifteen feet from the elevator was a guard station. Inside were two armed guards, fourteen security monitors, etc. Behind the guard station were sleeping quarters, where two other guards rested on their break. This was connected to the other guard station at the far end of the ward. On either side, there were six large cells, each one with an electronically locked steel door. There were two other large cells at the back of the ward. That's where my client was.

Captain Wills spoke to the two guards and was given a small metal box by one. Inside were two pair of black glasses (goggles, really), the kind they wear to watch a nuclear blast or something of that nature. He handed me a pair and said, "You'll need these once you're inside with your client." When we got to the cell door, he told me to put the glasses on. I did as he suggested, and everything went black. He said, "It will take a few minutes for your eyes to adjust, and once you're inside, they'll have to adjust again."

He took out an electronic key card and slid it in the slot by the door. After a series of clicks, the door opened. The light from the cell was so bright that even with the dark glasses on, your eyes automatically squeezed shut. As the door shut behind us, my eyes slowly adjusted. Everywhere you looked, you saw bright white light. The walls and ceiling were really solar light panels.

Captain Wills said, "If you don't wear the glasses in here, you'd go blind."

At the cell's center was a table about four and a half feet long by three feet wide and three chairs. Off to one side was a bathroom. On the other side, there was a bed, a closet, a nightstand, and a bookshelf. On the bed sat my client.

"Welcome to my humble abode, Mr. Afina." He stood up and extended his hand.

I shook it and motioned for him to join me at the table. Captain Wills said he'd be back in an hour or so and took his leave. My client was dressed in an orange jumpsuit (prison issue), sneakers, and—of course—dark glasses.

"So, Mr. Afina, what's new on the home front?"

"Well," I said, "tomorrow we go before the judge at the preliminary hearing to enter a plea and, if possible, set bail. Also, I do have a few more questions for you, Mr. Damon."

"First off, Mr. Afina," he said, "cut the Mister crap and call me Charles. Secondly, I know you've seen the video, so what do you think my chances are?" He caught me off guard with that, but I tried to remain cool.

"How do you know about that?" I asked.

"This is a prison after all," he said. "People talk, especially the guards."

"Okay, Charles, but before we go any further, I'll ask you again. Did you kill those people?"

He looked at me and said, "The world is full of possibilities." Then he added, "Would you drop my case if I say I did?"

I said, "As your lawyer, I can't." Then I went into the whole spiel about anything told to me in confidence coming under the heading of lawyer-client privilege and that anything he said stayed in the room with us. As I was saying, this I was also observing Charles. He wasn't loud or pretentious like most of my clients. He was cool, calm, and very crafty. "To answer your question about your chances," I said, "the judge will probably deny bail after seeing that video tape." I watched for a reaction to this statement, but there wasn't any. We could have been talking about the weather for all his concern.

Then he said, "It doesn't matter." When I asked why, Charles's expression was like, "Surely, you jest."

"If you believe what your eyes have seen, how long do you think they can hold me?" As he spoke, I didn't believe his pulse sped up one beat—a real cold customer.

"Anyway," I said, "how did you know the speaker at the convention hall?"

"I used to work for him," Charles said. "He's the CEO—excuse me—*was* the CEO of Digicom. Up until three months ago, I designed digital microcomputers for them."

"What happened three months ago?" I asked.

He gave me that dumbfounded look again, and then he did something strange. He smiled. It was the smile of someone who looked down at a chessboard and knew his opponent was beaten. The smile of a Michael Jordan as he watched his three-pointer fly through the air, knowing it was all net. The smile of someone with a huge and terrible secret. Just as quickly as his expression had changed, it went back to normal, blank and cold. Then he said, "It doesn't matter now. What time will I be going to court tomorrow?"

"The hearing is scheduled for nine a.m.," I said.

Before I could pursue the matter of his relationship, or lack thereof, with his late employer any further, Captain Wills entered. He pulled me to the side and informed me I had an urgent call from the chief of police. I turned to Charles Damon and told him I had to leave and would see him in the morning at the hearing. Then Captain Wills and I left.

Once outside the cell, we took off our goggles and waited for our eyes to adjust. Captain Wills had the call transferred from his office to the guard station. When I took the phone, I was greeted by the chief of police. He said that the doctor who claimed to have information about Mr. Damon was there with him now and that I should get there as soon as possible. I informed him that I would be on my way as soon as our conversation ended.

An hour later, I was driving downtown to One Police Plaza. Before going to see my client, I had left several messages for the police chief. Apparently, he was out trying to find this mysterious doctor. As soon as I entered the building, I was led straight to his office. The officer knocked on the door, and we were told to come in. The chief was seated behind his deck, which had two chairs in front of it. One was empty. The other was occupied by a man in his late fifties or early sixties.

"Hello, Mr. Afina," the chief said as he stood up. "Glad you could make it on such short notice. Please have a seat and we'll get right down to business."

I said, "Thanks for inviting me," and I took the empty seat. "Mr. Afina, allow me to introduce you to Dr. Albert Martin."

I turned toward the elderly man, extending my hand, and said, "Hello, Doctor."

He shook my hand and said he was pleased to meet me, even under these circumstances. For a man his age, he had a nice, firm grip. The chief reached into his desk drawer and pulled out a tape recorder.

"This conversation will have to be taped," he said. I replied, "Yes, I understand."

"Well, Dr. Martin," he said, "let us begin." With that said, he turned on the tape recorder.

"For the record, my name is Dr. Albert Martin. I am here because I believe I'm the only living person with any knowledge of Charles Damon's past. In 1980, I was working in a hospital in Texas, doing my graduate studies for my PhD in genetics. That is the year Mr. Damon was born. The only reason I became aware of Charles Damon at all is because of two strange things that happened. The day after his birth, his mother died. Due to the fact his mother was a Navajo Indian and his father was black, certain things were looked for during the autopsy—drug use, alcohol abuse, sickle cell anemia, high blood pressure, diabetes, heart disease, and cancer. All these things were ruled out as the cause of death. What she died of was fright. She was literally scared to death.

"Due to the lack of cause and the strangeness of her death, I was asked to analyze her blood for any abnormalities. I found nothing that would explain her death, but I did find something strange. She had an altered gene. I expressed this in my written and verbal reports, but it was dismissed since it couldn't account for the cause of death. The hospital board was more worried about a lawsuit. I also did a blood analysis on the baby. He too had an altered gene. One week later, after exhausting questions and legal paperwork, the father was allowed to take Charles home.

"I kept in touch with Charles Senior since we had become acquainted during the investigation of his wife's death. He allowed me to test his blood also, thinking that he might lose his son. I found no mutation in his genetic structure, but I found minute traces of radiation in his blood. When I asked him about his background, he said he worked for an oil company. He studied core samples to see if the drill site would produce oil. I didn't tell him about the radiation in his blood cells. I wasn't sure if it meant anything yet, and he had enough on his plate.

"Two weeks later, he was dead. The police found him hanging from the rafters in his attic, baby Charles in a blanket lying at his feet. The official report was suicide. They said the strain of losing his wife and being a single parent was just too much for him. The unofficial report was that something had scared him so bad that he hung himself. His facial expression was the same as his wife's—sheer terror. Little Charles was placed in an orphanage, since neither parent had any living relatives. For the next fourteen years, I kept a discreet eye on Charles, out of scientific curiosity for the most part and also out of a sense of obligation to his father.

"In 1994, the orphanage burned to the ground. The only survivor, Charles Damon. Two things sensationalized the fire: the fact that no cause for it could be found, no accelerant, no faulty wiring, no gas leak, no overturned candles or careless cigarette smoke, nothing. It was like the house just burst into flames. Also, even though the other forty-four bodies were burned beyond recognition, it was discovered that some were ripped apart before they burned up. Charles became a ward of the state then and was placed in a foster home. Two weeks later, he disappeared. I couldn't find out anything about him until now. I had a theory back then, which I kept to myself. I continued to follow up on the information I had gathered about the Damon family. I needed facts to back up my theory, and over the years, I got them." Stopping for a moment, Dr. Martin looked at his watch. It was an hour and a half already. He said, "I haven't spoken this long since my lecture days in the late nineties, Chief," he said. "Can I possibly get

something to drink, preferably water?"

"Sure," the chief said. "I can use a cup of coffee myself." He turned and asked, "Anything for you, Mr. Afina?"

"Coffee, black with sugar," I said.

After the drinks were brought in, the doctor started to resume his story when the lights went out, not just the lights in the office or even the building, but also the lights all over the city. The emergency lights came on and then went out also.

The chief pulled out a battery-powered lantern and clicked it on. "I keep a few of these around just in case, you know, since the brownouts of the nineties."

"Chief!" the doctor exclaimed in a voice laden with fear. "If there is any way you can contact the prison, you better do it, fast! You've seen what Charles Damon can do in a normally lit room. Imagine what he's capable of in total darkness."

The chief pulled out a walkie-talkie from his desk and tried to contact the warden. After a minute or so, the warden's voice came through. "Hello!" he yelled. "Who is it?"

"Warden, this is the chief of police. Due to the current situation, I advise you to gas all the prisoners, ASAP."

"It's too late," the warden cried over ever-loudening noises in the background. "Prisoner Damon has escaped."

We could hear the walkie-talkie hit the floor as the warden screamed in terror. And we could finally make out the noise in the background. It was the screams of men being torn apart, the howls of wild animals, the roar of monsters, the sounds of death.